Usborne
Little First Stickers

Love and Kindness

· Illustrated by Kathryn Selbert ·

Written by Holly Bathie
Designed by Meg Dobbie

You'll find all the stickers
at the back of the book.

Little Acorn Village

A Squirrel family is moving into the treehouse in Little Acorn Village. They will need some help from their kind new neighbours to find their way around. Add more stickers to help them get to know everyone.

The Foxes

The Rabbits

The Badgers

The Bears

The Beavers

Hello Squirrels!

Welcome to our village. We love living here and we hope you will too.

Love the Foxes, Rabbits Badgers, Bears and Beavers. xx

Meet the Squirrel family

Stick on all the members of the Squirrel family. They are leaving their treehouse in Ferny Forest to move to their new home in Little Acorn Village.

Mum and Dad
feel lucky that so many kind people will help them move.

Sammy
is looking forward to making new friends.

Sylvester
hopes Granny and Grandad will come to visit their new home.

Suki
is feeling a bit unsure. She has little bunny to cuddle.

Friends forever

The little squirrels are feeling a bit sad about saying goodbye to Ferny Forest, but their lovely friends have made them cards to show how much they care. Finish decorating the cards with stickers.

GOOD LUCK!

HAPPY NEW HOME

·ENJOY YOUR NEW HOME·

The Squirrels
The Treehouse
Big Oak Tree
Little Acorn Village

A special welcome

Just as the Squirrels have unloaded all their things, there's a knock at the door. The Bears have come to say hello. Stick on friendly Mr Bear with a tasty pie.

The families in the village have planned a surprise for the Squirrels. Decorate the invitation with stickers.

· · · · · · · ·

Please come to our picnic to welcome you to Little Acorn Village.

It's today at 2pm at Picnic Place.

There will be lots of food, and games too!

· · · · · · · ·

Picnic time

The animals have gathered to share their lunch and make the Squirrels feel welcome. Each family has made something for the picnic table. Stick on lots of yummy food, and a little beaver who has eaten too much.

Bedtime

What a lovely day it's been! Now the little squirrels are warm and comfy in their beds, looking forward to living in Little Acorn Village with their kind new friends. Add more stickers to this cosy scene.